Jake the Philharmonic DOG

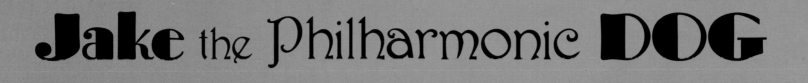

Karen LeFrak
Illustrations by Marcin Baranski

WALKER & COMPANY
New York

1/07

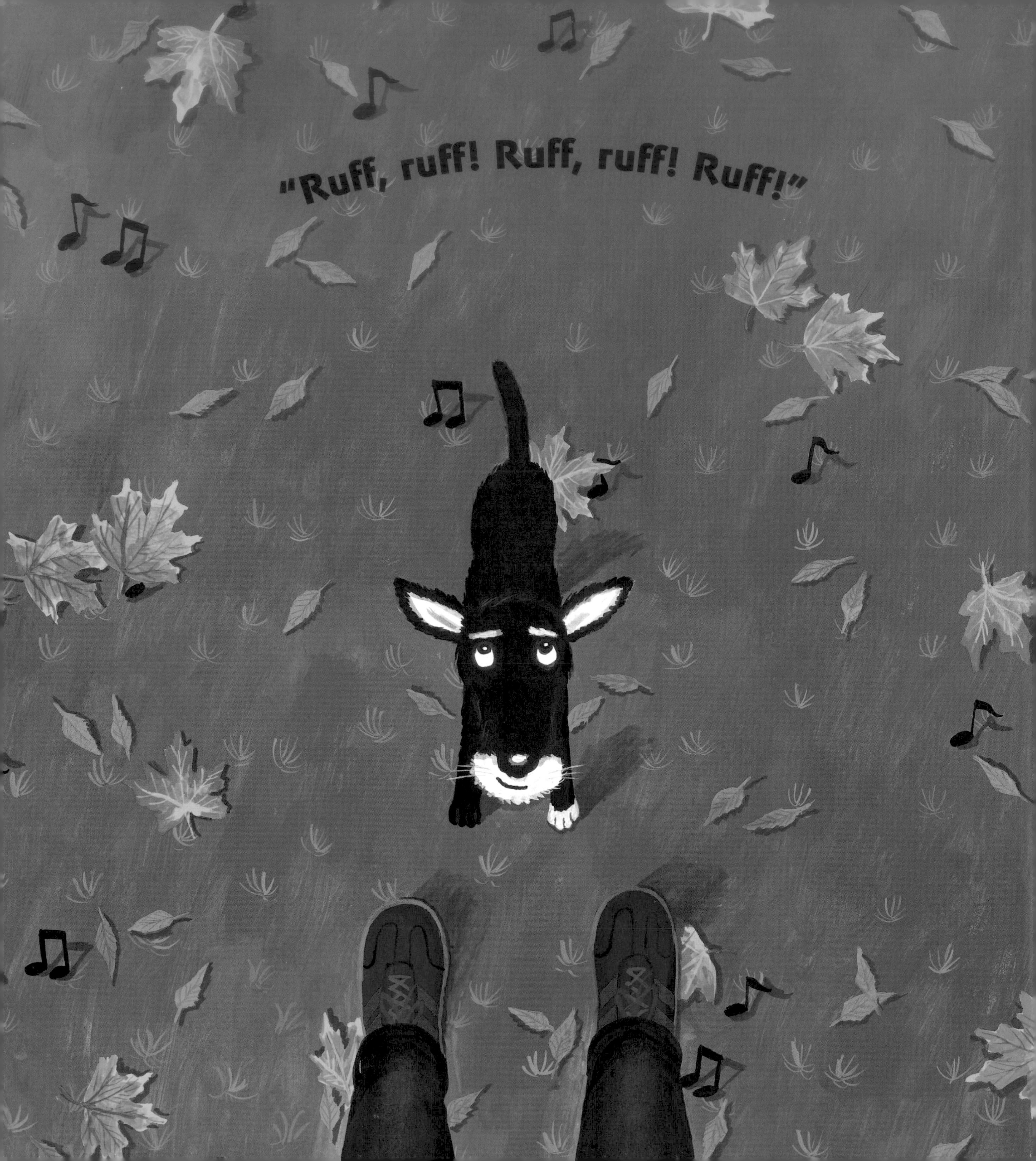
"Ruff, ruff! Ruff, ruff! Ruff!"

Richie thought the small black dog sounded like he was singing. One look at the little fellow swishing his tail back and forth was enough for Richie to know this was the perfect dog for him.

Jake's musical barking and rhythmic tail wagging reminded him of something else he loved: his job as principal stagehand for the Philharmonic Orchestra.

Jake and Richie did a lot of things together. Jake loved going to the park with Richie to play fetch.

"Tweet! Tweet!" As birds chirped in a nest high above, Jake threw his head back and answered, **"Woof! Woof! Woof!"**

Jake and Richie also loved long car rides.

"Honk!"

"Ruff!"

"Honk!"

"Ruff!"

Jake answered each honking car. His tail moved back and forth, back and forth, like windshield wipers.

But there was one sound that Jake didn't like: THUNDER. The first time the sky grew black and lightning flashed across it, followed by a **BOOM,** Jake's ears flattened. He went around and around in circles, his tail between his legs.

"Hey, pal! Do you want to play fetch?" Richie threw a rolled up newspaper, but Jake didn't notice.

"Jake! Want a biscuit, boy?" Richie rattled the box of special treats, but
Jake just whimpered.

Richie didn't know what to do. Music usually helped him think, so
he turned on the CD player. The sound of violins streamed through the air.
Suddenly, Jake cocked his head and started thumping his tail, back and
forth, back and forth.

"There you go. That's better, isn't it?" said Richie, gently scratching Jake behind his ears. "Who knew you liked music so much? You know what? I'm going to take you to work with me tomorrow!" And they shook on it—hand and paw.

The next day, Richie and Jake drove to the grand concert hall. Jake lifted

his ears as he entered the backstage area. So many new sounds! So many

new scents! His eyes swiveled as a sea of legs weaved around him.

Jake looked proudly at Richie as he set up chairs and music stands on the stage, putting sheets of music on each one.

The musicians took the stage and they all found their seats. Suddenly,

someone was kneeling by Jake, giving him the neck rub of his life!

"Jake, this is Glenn," said Richie. "He's the concertmaster. He'll run the

rehearsal until the conductor arrives."

"Tweet! Tweet!"

Then birdsong seemed to fill the air. Jake threw back his head. **"Woof! Woof! Woof!"**

But just as quickly as it had begun, the bird melody stopped. The only sound now was Richie's laughter.

"Jake!" Richie said. "There aren't any birds here, boy. That's the flute players warming up. They're part of the woodwind section of the orchestra."

The musicians all looked down. "Jake!" Richie patted him on the head.
"That's not a *car* horn. That's a *French* horn! See? The brass instruments are
warming up now!"

Xylophone

Gong

Triangle

Cymbals

Bass drum

Timpani

Richie knew what was coming next—but before he could
say a word, a drumroll started, quiet at first, then swelling
louder and louder, followed by **CRASH! BOOM!**

"Arrrhmmm! Arrrhmmm!" Jake whimpered.

Everyone in the orchestra froze and watched wide-eyed

as Jake turned quick circles offstage, his tail between his legs.

"Jake! Jake! It's not thunder, boy! It's not! It's just the

percussion section!" Richie called out, but Jake didn't stop

running in circles.

"Glenn, quick! Have the string section play something. Anything!"

Glenn signaled to the musicians, and the strings began to play.

As soon as he heard the soothing sound of violins, Jake sat up straight and listened. His tail now wagged back and forth, back and forth.

"Good boy, Jake! The string section is your favorite, isn't it, pal?" Richie said, scratching Jake behind the ears.

As Glenn stepped to the podium, Richie said, "Listen to how all these instruments sound together when they play in the orchestra!"

Jake cocked his head as Glenn began to wave his arms at the orchestra. Why was he trying to shoo them away? Jake wondered. But then, the most wonderful sound filled the air as the whole orchestra played together. Even Jake knew to keep quiet.

Richie put a cushion in the wings so Jake could have his own special place
to sit while the musicians played. As the rehearsal was going well, Richie
said, "Come on, buddy, let's go for a walk in the park before the concert."

By the time they returned to the hall, Jake was kind of sleepy.

"I'll be back in a minute, boy. I just need to take care of a few things," Richie said.

Jake wandered lazily across the empty stage, waiting for Richie, sniffing a chair here, a music stand there. When he reached the podium, Jake saw something that perked him up a bit. A stick! Jake took it and wandered off the stage to find Richie so they could play fetch.

But there was Jake's plump new cushion, and he couldn't resist it. He yawned. The stick fell from his mouth and rolled behind the cushion. Then Jake curled up and took a nap.

The sound of the orchestra warming up woke Jake a short time later. As he stretched, someone he'd never seen before walked onto the stage. The audience clapped, and the musicians picked up their instruments. The man went to the podium and bowed to the audience. Everyone was quiet.

But then the man began to search the podium, looking for something.

"Oh, no!" said Richie. "The baton! I know I put it out before we went to the park. What's happened to it?"

Jake watched as everyone began to fidget—the orchestra and the audience. He took the opportunity to meet the new person and try to start a game of fetch.

Jake nosed behind the cushion, got his stick, and trotted out onto the stage before Richie realized what was happening.

"Bravo! Bravo!" The audience burst into wild applause upon seeing Jake
with the baton in his mouth.

The conductor raised an eyebrow at his surprise guest. Then he turned, bowed to the little dog, and took the baton from his mouth. The audience rose to their feet and cheered.

Jake was so happy that his tail began to wag, back and forth, back and forth. The conductor watched, then raised the baton and followed Jake's beat. He turned to the orchestra to start the music. The audience quickly took their seats. Jake scurried off to the wings to take his. And Jake's first official concert began.

Coda

From then on, Jake came to work with Richie every day. After all, the principal stagepaw had to bring the conductor his baton at the start of each performance.

♪ Musical Notes ♪

♪ **Baton**: A baton is a thin stick used by a conductor to set the beat for musicians. But if you were Jake and didn't know that, you'd just think it was a good stick for playing fetch!

♪ **Beat**: A beat is a sound repeated at regular intervals. Jake's tail is always beating, back and forth, back and forth.

♪ **Brass**: A section of the orchestra featuring instruments made from metal that produce a tone when musicians buzz their lips in a special mouthpiece.

♪ **Bravo**: An audience cries "Bravo!" to show that they like the performance they have just seen and/or heard.

♪ **Coda**: *Coda* is an Italian word that means "tail." In music it means an extra ending.

♪ **Concertmaster**: A concertmaster, like Glenn, is the leader of the first violin section of an orchestra. He tunes up the orchestra and helps get them ready to play.

♪ **Conductor**: A conductor is in charge of an orchestra. The conductor helps musicians know how and when to play their parts and how to bring all the sounds of the orchestra's instruments together.

♪ **Melody**: A melody is a series of musical notes that make up a tune. Jake's barking is Richie's favorite melody.

♪ **Percussion**: A section of the orchestra featuring instruments that are struck, shaken, or scraped to produce a tone or set the beat for all the instruments.

♪ **Philharmonic orchestra**: An orchestra is a group of musicians who play music together. The word *philharmonic* actually means "loving harmony." The core of an orchestra is made up of the four main sections and core instruments Jake has learned about. Other instruments, such as the piano, harp, piccolo, and English horn, can also play with the orchestra.

♪ **Stagehand**: A stagehand is someone who works behind the scenes at a theater or concert hall and makes sure that everything on stage is set up right. A principal stagehand, like Richie, is the stagehand in charge.

♪ **Strings**: A section of the orchestra featuring four-stringed wooden instruments of different sizes that are either plucked or played with a bow.

♪ **Woodwinds**: A section of the orchestra featuring instruments that produce a tone by blowing into them and covering various holes to make different notes.

To "Ruffle," without whom I would not
know how to hear the music in Jake
—K. L.

To my brother Andrzej —M. B.

Text copyright © 2006 by Karen LeFrak
Illustrations copyright © 2006 by Marcin Baranski

First published in the United States of America in 2006 by
Walker Publishing Company, Inc.
Distributed to the trade by Holtzbrinck Publishers

For information about permission to reproduce selections from
this book, write to Permissions, Walker & Company,
104 Fifth Avenue, New York, New York 10011.

Library of Congress Cataloging-in-Publication Data
LeFrak, Karen.
Jake the philharmonic dog / Karen LeFrak ; illustrated by Marcin Baranski.
p. cm.
ISBN-10: 0-8027-9552-8 (hardcover)
ISBN-13: 978-0-8027-9552-6 (hardcover)
ISBN-10: 0-8027-9553-6 (reinforced)
ISBN-13: 978-0-8027-9553-3 (reinforced)
1. Dogs—Juvenile literature. 2. Orchestra—Juvenile literature.
I. Baranski, Marcin. II. Title.
SF426.5L44 2006   636.7—dc22   2006000473

The artist used acrylic and tempera paint on Bristol paper to create the
illustrations for this book.

Book design by Nicole Gastonguay

Visit Walker & Company's Web site at www.walkeryoungreaders.com

Printed in China

10 9 8 7 6 5 4 3 2 1

ACKNOWLEDGMENTS:

I offer special thanks to my wonderful literary agent, Fredrica
Friedman, and outstanding editor and publisher, Emily Easton.
My appreciation goes to the philharmonic musicians and staff,
in particular Eric Latzky, and to all my fellow dog lovers,
especially Wendell Sammet, Barbara Green, and Thea Feldman.
I want to recognize Marcin Baranski for his delightful illustrations
and T. Byram Karasu for his tireless encouragement. I also wish
to thank my supportive family Richard, Harry, and Jamie. A
great big thank you to Jake and his family, Richie Norton and
Suzie Forzano, who should all take a bow. Wow!

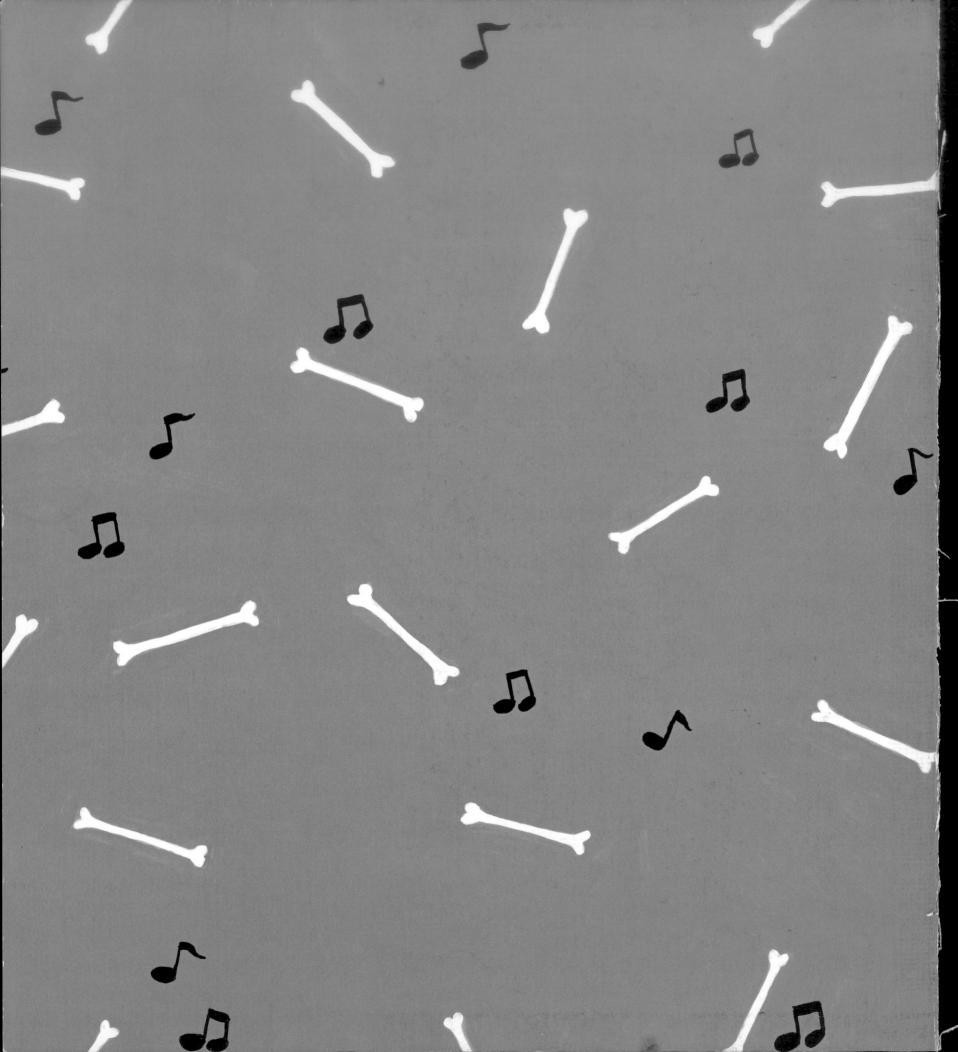